This Little Tiger
book belongs to:

_____

_____

LITTLE
TIGER PRESS
1 The Coda Centre,
189 Munster Road,
London SW6 6AW
www.littletiger.co.uk

First published in
Great Britain 2014

Text by Mara Alperin
Text copyright © Little Tiger Press 2014
Illustrations copyright © Kate Daubney 2014
Kate Daubney has asserted her right to be
identified as the illustrator of this work
under the Copyright, Designs and Patents Act, 1988
A CIP catalogue record for this book is
available from the British Library

ISBN 978-1-84895-683-4
Printed in China
LTP/1400/0756/1013
2 4 6 8 10 9 7 5 3 1

To Katie Thompson, whose EasyBake cookies
were always just right ~ M A

For Roger. Artist, adventurer and my ally ~ K D

Mara Alperin · Kate Daubney

Goldilocks
and the
Three Bears

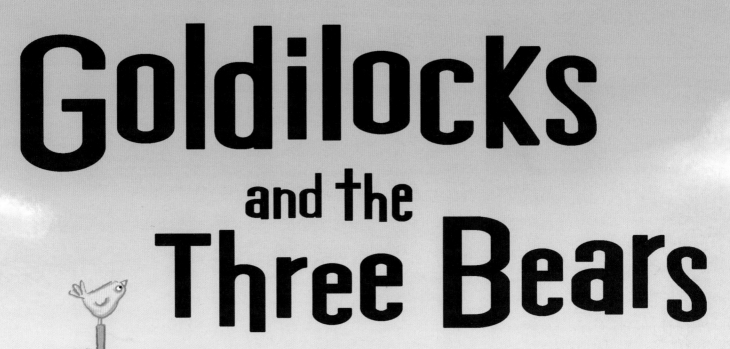

LITTLE TIGER PRESS
London

Once there were three bears who lived
together in a cosy, little cottage. Each
morning, they made yummy-scrummy
porridge for breakfast – it was the
best meal of the day!

But one morning, Baby Bear said,
"Ouch! This porridge is
hot-hot-hot!"

"Let's take a walk before
breakfast and give it time to cool,"
said Mummy Bear. And so they did.

No sooner had the bears left than someone peeked in through the window – someone with bright, golden hair. Her name was Goldilocks … and she was a **very** cheeky little girl!

BEST OATS

For a Beary Good Breakfast

Goldilocks tap-tap-**tapped** on the door.
"Hello?" she called.
"Helloooo?"

When no answer came, she pushed the door open and crept inside to explore.

What a delicious smell!

Goldilocks
tiptoed into the
kitchen and saw three bowls
of yummy-scrummy porridge
on the table.

She slurped Daddy Bear's porridge, but it was too lumpy.

She sipped Mummy Bear's porridge, but it was too sweet.

Then she tasted Baby Bear's porridge. It was

just right...

...so she ate it all up!

Goldilocks was very full, so she looked around for somewhere to sit. There in the sitting room were three **magnificent** chairs.

She tried Daddy Bear's chair, but it was too **hard**.

Then she rocked in Baby Bear's chair. It was just right ...

She squished into Mummy Bear's chair, but it was too soft.

"Wheee!" cried Goldilocks. She rocked and rocked, faster and faster, until ...

CRASH!

went the chair, and broke into a hundred pieces. "Oopsie!" giggled Goldilocks.

She was having SO much fun! "I wonder what's upstairs?" she said.

Up in the bedroom were three **wonderful** beds.

Goldilocks jumped on Daddy Bear's bed, but it was too squeaky.

She bounced on Mummy Bear's bed, but it was *too squashy*.

Then she hopped to Baby Bear's bed.

It was just right ...

"ZZZZZZZZZZZZZZ!"

snored Goldilocks.
She had fallen fast asleep!

But as Goldilocks slept on, the three bears came home. They were very, **very** hungry. And when they opened the door . . .

"Someone's been eating my porridge," growled Daddy Bear.

"Someone's been
eating my porridge,"
rumbled Mummy Bear.

"Someone's been eating
my porridge," cried
Baby Bear. "And now
it's all gone!"

And before Mummy Bear could make some more porridge, they heard a loud **ROAR** from the sitting room.

"Someone's been sitting in my chair," growled Daddy Bear.

"Someone's been sitting in my chair," rumbled Mummy Bear, rushing over.

"Someone's been sitting in my chair," cried Baby Bear. "And now it's broken!"

But before Daddy Bear could fix the chair,
they all heard a noise coming from above.
One after the other, the three
bears crept up the stairs . . .

"Someone's been sleeping in my bed," growled Daddy Bear.

"Someone's been sleeping in my bed," rumbled Mummy Bear.

"Someone's been sleeping in my bed!" cried Baby Bear …

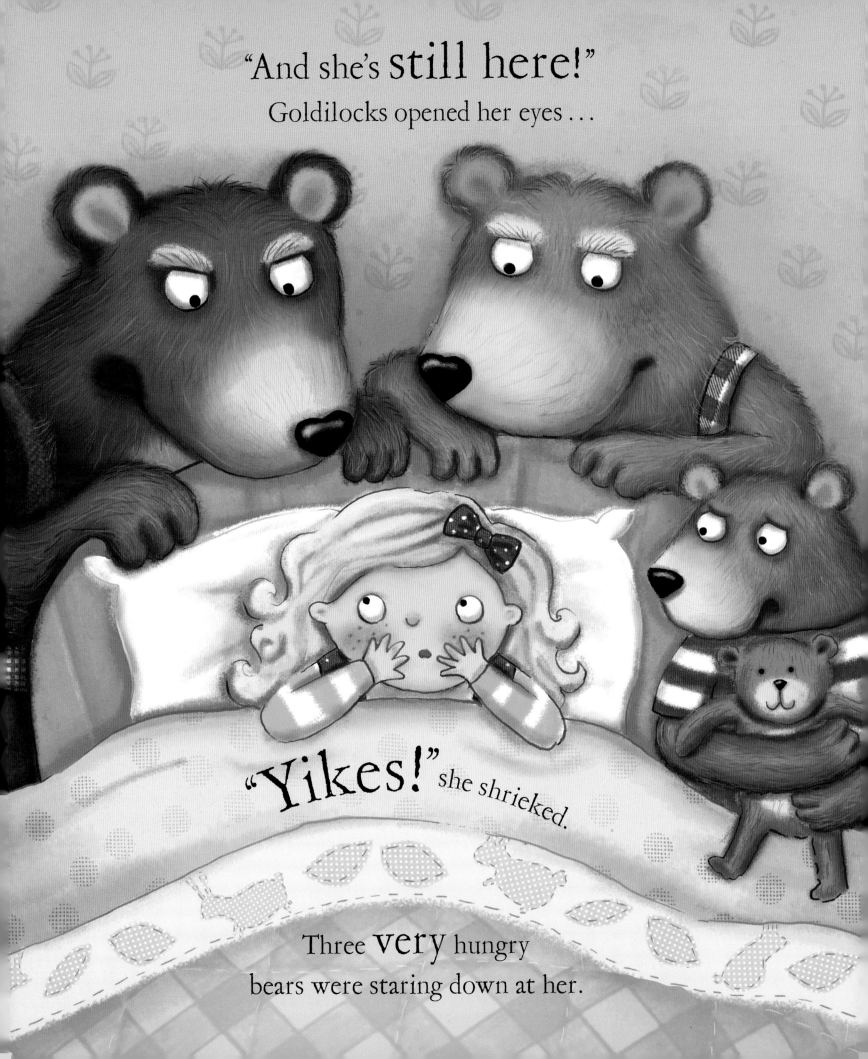

Goldilocks leaped up
and dashed down
the stairs . . .

. . . and bumped into
the kitchen table.

SMACK!
The bowls of
porridge flew
up, up up . . .

. . . and the gooey porridge fell
SPLAT onto her
golden hair!
"Ewwwww!"
yelped Goldilocks.

The last the three bears saw of Goldilocks
was her dashing down the path,
leaving a very sticky trail
of porridge behind her.

"Someone's covered in yummy-scrummy
porridge," growled Daddy Bear.
"Someone's covered in licky-sticky honey,"
tutted Mummy Bear.
"Can we have toast for breakfast
instead?" said Baby Bear.
And so they did!

Collect every one!

My First Fairy Tales are familiar, fun and friendly stories – with a marvellously modern twist!

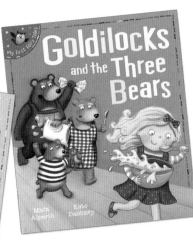

Psssst! coming soon!

The Three Little Pigs

The Gingerbread Man

Chicken Licken

Rumpelstiltskin